THE
MAGNIFICENT
MUMMIES

TONY BRADMAN
MARTIN CHATTERTON

Blue Bananas

For Bindi
T.B.

For Sophie and Danny
M.C.

THE
MAGNIFICENT
MUMMIES

TONY BRADMAN
MARTIN CHATTERTON

HEINEMANN

Titles in the series:

Big Dog and Little Dog Visit the Moon
The Nut Map
Dilly and the Goody-Goody
Tom's Hats
Juggling with Jeremy
Baby Bear Comes Home
The Magnificent Mummies
Mouse Flute
Delilah Digs for Treasure
Owl in the House
Runaway Fred
Keeping Secrets

First published in Great Britain 1997
by Heinemann and Mammoth, imprints of Reed International Books Ltd
Michelin House, 81 Fulham Road, London SW3 6RB
and Auckland, Melbourne, Singapore and Toronto
Text copyright © Tony Bradman 1997
Illustrations copyright © Martin Chatterton 1997
The Author and Illustrator have asserted their moral rights
Paperback ISBN 0 7497 2767 5
Hardback ISBN 0 434 97482 X
1 3 5 7 9 10 8 6 4 2
A CIP catalogue record for this title
is available from the British Library
Produced by Mandarin Offset Ltd
Printed and bound in China

Far away in the Land of Sand . . .

. . .there flows a big, slow river.

(Who's that swimming in it?

Oh, never mind.)

By that big, slow river,

there stands a pyramid.

(Who's that putting up a sign?

Oh, never mind.)

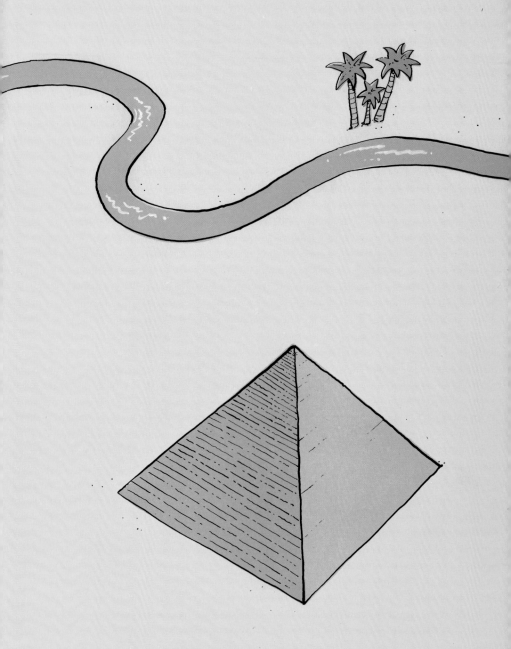

And inside that pyramid you'll find...

. . . a family of mummies.

And here they are to say hello!

The Mummies were having a quiet, restful day. Mummy Mummy was reading the paper. Daddy Mummy was cooking in the kitchen. And the Mummy kids were watching TV.

11

The Mummy family sat down at the
table. Tut and Sis were soon
in trouble.

They were saved by a

loud knocking noise!

KNOCK KNOCK

The knocking went on,

and on,

and on.

So the Mummies went to the front door.

Daddy Mummy opened the door and

the Mummies peered out.

16

A man was standing outside.

The man didn't say anything. He just went
very pale . . . and fainted dead away.

They brought him in, and brought him round. The man soon got over his surprise. His name was Sir Digby Digger. He was an archaeologist, so he did lots of digging. The Mummies asked Sir Digby to stay to tea. They laughed and joked and became great friends.

But at last it was time

for Sir Digby to go.

19

The Mummies gave Sir Digby some old
things they didn't need any more.

He seemed quite pleased.

Then they took him

to the front door.

Sir Digby climbed into his car... but he didn't get very far.

His car made an odd coughing noise.

Sir Digby's car just wouldn't start!

Sir Digby lost his temper.

Sir Digby kicked his car, very hard.

The Mummy family and Sir Digby tried

to mend the car. But it was no use.

All it did was cough, cough, cough.

Sir Digby was rather upset.

He had an important appointment

at a monument in Memphis.

'It's at eight, and

I mustn't be late!'

said Sir Digby.

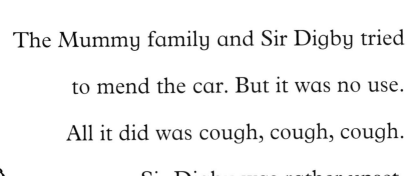

Bags I be... the mechanic!

Then Mummy Mummy

had a brilliant idea.

Mummy Mummy led the way.

They all went round the corner,

and round the corner again.

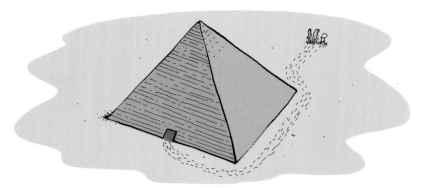

And there was the place Mummy

Mummy had seen in the paper.

The two Sheikhs were called Rattle and
Roll and they were very helpful.
Sir Digby chose a camel
and paid for it.

The camel left quite quickly.

The Mummies waved goodbye.

'What shall we do now?'

'The washing, I think. You need some

clean bandages!' said Mummy Mummy.

So they
collected
the dirty
washing
and headed
for the river.
But when
they arrived,
they couldn't
believe their
eyes. The
river had
vanished.
What a surprise!

The Mummies were stumped.

They stood on the sand of the river bank

and looked down at more...sand.

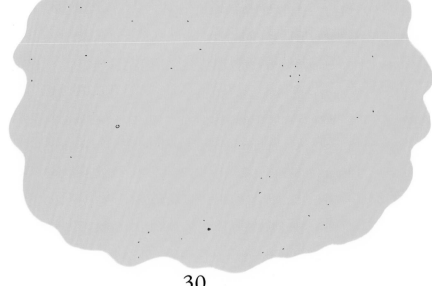

The Mummies set off to investigate.

Tut and Sis ran ahead.

But they soon came

racing back.

Tut and Sis were both very

excited. They dragged

Mummy Mummy and

Daddy Mummy

along by the hands.

31

And there it was...

The BIGGEST creature they

had ever seen.

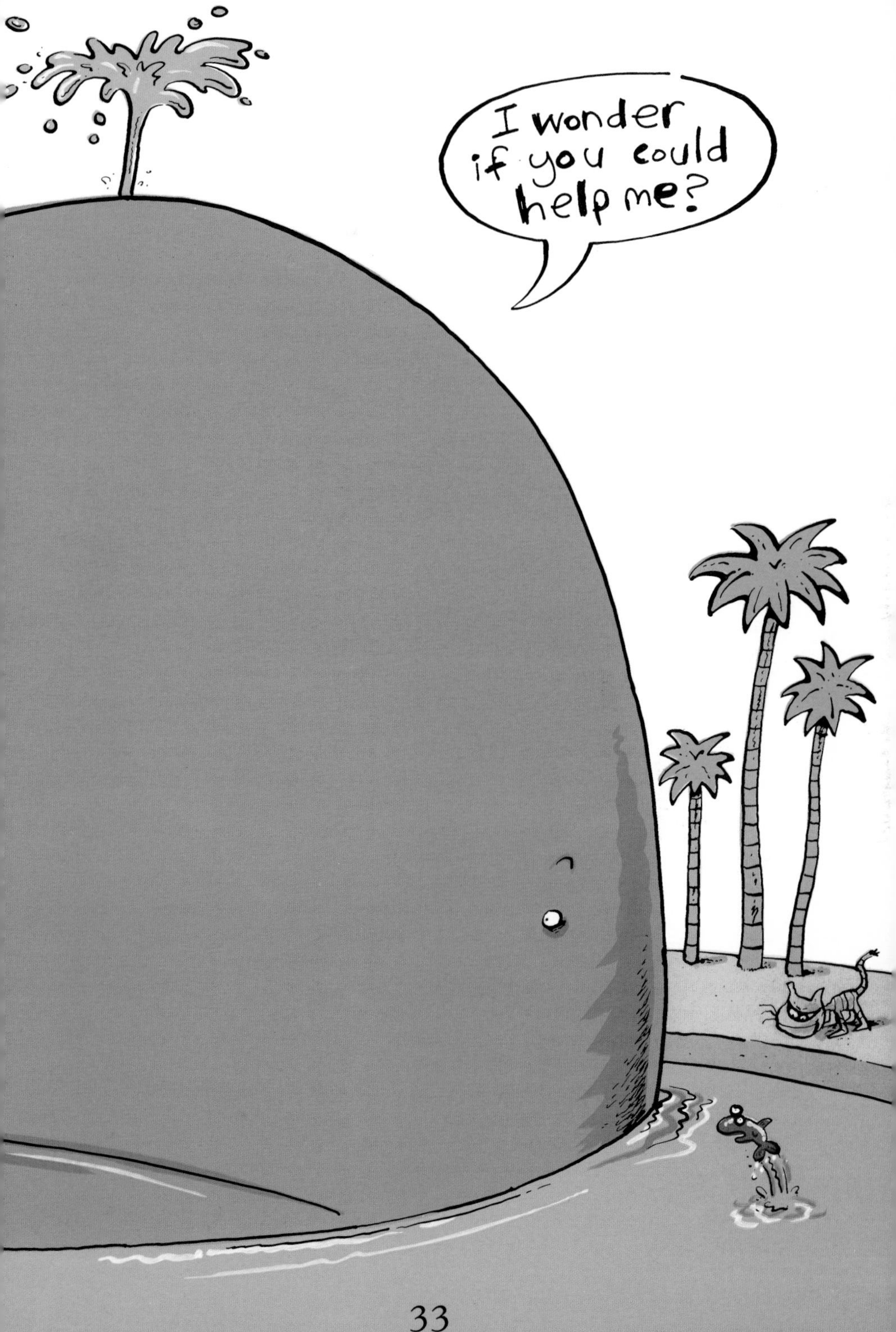
I wonder if you could help me?

It was a huge whale, and his name was
Moby. He had got lost, and swum into the
river by mistake. Now he was stuck fast
where the river had started to grow
narrow . . .

. . . and none of the water could flow past.

Poor Moby looked very unhappy.

Then Daddy Mummy had a brilliant
idea!

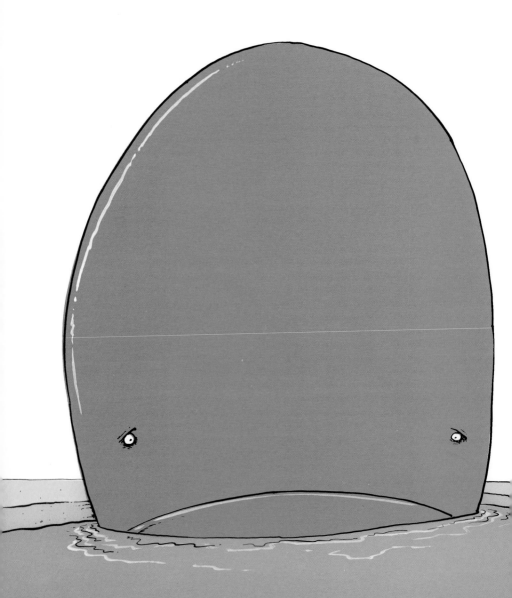

They needed someone who was

good at digging!

And they knew just the man for the job!

Daddy Mummy sent Tut and Sis

dashing to the Used Camel

Lot with a message.

Minutes later a cloud of dust left

the pyramid.

Inside it were the Two Sheikhs.

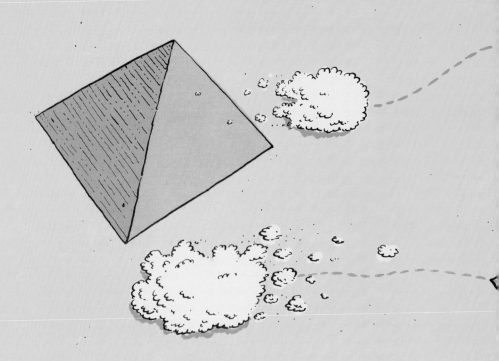

Soon a slightly bigger cloud of dust

returned. Inside that were the Two

Sheikhs... and Sir Digby Digger!

But Sir Digby was a man with a plan.

40

He drew some lines in the sand...

and got everybody digging

and digging

and digging.

The river came flooding back. And
now there was a great big pool of lovely
cool water, too. Moby was free!
He was very pleased.
So he made sure that Sir
Digby and the Two
Sheikhs and the
Mummies had
a whale of
a time!

The Mummies even got

the washing done.

At last, the sun started to set,

and it was time to go.

Sir Digby went...

 the Two Sheikhs went. . .

Moby went...

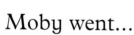

and the Mummy family went as well.

On the way home, they were so happy,

they did the famous Mummy sand

dance by the light of the moon.

It had been a wonderful day in the Land of Sand.

And now the Mummies were very tired.

And that's the end of the story.

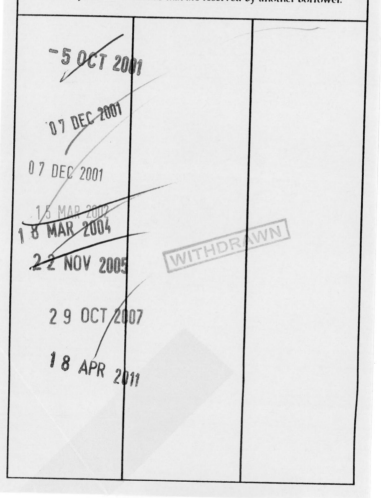